The Corridor

CW00881922

Titles in Teen Reads:

Badger Publishing Limited, Oldmedow Road, Hardwick Industrial Estate, King's Lynn PE30 4JJ
Telephone: 01438 791037

www.badgerlearning.co.uk

THE CORRIDOR

MARK WRIGHT

The Corridor ISBN 978-1-78147-573-7

Text © Mark Wright 2014
Complete work © Badger Publishing Limited 2014

All rights reserved. No part of this publication may be
reproduced, stored in any form or by any means mechanical,
electronic, recording or otherwise without the prior permission
of the publisher.

The right of Mark Wright to be identified as author of this Work has
been asserted by him in accordance with the Copyright, Designs and
Patents Act 1988.

Publisher: Susan Ross
Senior Editor: Danny Pearson
Copyeditor: Cheryl Lanyon
Designer: Bigtop Design Ltd
Printed by Bell and Bain Ltd, Glasgow

2 4 6 8 10 9 7 5 3

CHAPTER 1

"We love it!"

Frances and her little brother, Tom, looked
up at the big house standing in front of them,
enormous grins on their faces. Mum and Dad
stood behind them, Dad's arms placed around
their shoulders.

"Really?" asked Dad. "You really like it?"

Mum laughed as they both shouted: "Yes!"

It was moving day for the Brooks family. The
large house, built from blackened stone and
looking out over a valley of green Yorkshire

fields, was to be their new home. It even had a name – Stancliffe House. Frances was excited and couldn't wait to move in. She and Tom had chosen their bedrooms. Now all they needed to do was shift the enormous pile of boxes littering the front lawn into the house to begin unpacking.

Mum picked up a box. "Come on, Tom, love, let's get these inside."

Tom wasn't listening. He'd climbed up onto the stone wall surrounding the garden and was sitting cross-legged, opening his book.

"I'll just finish this chapter."

The tip of his tongue stuck out in concentration as he lost himself in yet another book about space, or time travel, or something. Frances loved her little brother, but sometimes he could be a pain.

"Tom, if you don't come and help, I'm going to nick your bedroom!"

Tom looked up and glared. "Don't you dare, Fran!" Frances laughed as he leapt from the wall and ran towards her.

"Got to catch me first!" she giggled, racing away across the lawn, dodging between two boxes.

"Hello," a voice called from down the lane. "Moving in today?"

"That's right," said Dad, greeting the lady who walked up to the wall. Frances thought she looked quite old with her grey hair and creased face, but she walked with a quick step and her blue eyes were bright.

"Kids, this is Mrs Gardner. She lives in the house at the bottom of the lane."

Mrs Gardner smiled. "And you two must be Frances and Tom?"

Frances said hello uncertainly. Tom just smiled shyly.

"I've been looking forward to meeting you both."
When the old lady looked at them, those bright
eyes sparkled mysteriously. "Do come and see
me whenever you like."

"OK," said Frances, not sure why she'd want to
go and see her.

Tom had gone back to his book. Mrs Gardner
said goodbye to the family and walked along the
lane. Before she disappeared around the side of
the house, she glanced at Frances one last time.
Then she was gone.

While Mum tried to get Tom to pull his nose out
of his book to lend a hand, Frances picked up a
box and struggled towards the house. It was the
box her iPod dock was packed in. Unpacking
boxes always needed music.

Frances nudged open the front door and stepped
inside Stancliffe House. The door opened onto
the large kitchen. It was nice and warm in
there. Although the house was old, it had been

modernised, bits of it rebuilt over the years, and she could hear the boiler for the central heating rumbling away in the distance. She lugged the box across the kitchen and through the door opposite.

Frances found herself in the long connecting corridor between the kitchen and the main house, leading towards the hallway and stairs. Stancliffe House was a maze of these long passageways that linked rooms. It wasn't one of those new-build houses. Mum said it had character and history, and Frances liked that.

Wooden floorboards shifted under her feet as Frances stepped along the passage. She'd have to put the box down at the other end, it was getting heavier by the second.

A chill suddenly passed through the corridor. Frances shivered and almost dropped the box. Then, she heard it. A whisper.

"Please..." It sounded like a breath. "Please..."

Goose bumps appeared on Frances's arms as the corridor turned even colder and the light seemed to dim, casting shadows all around her.

"Who's there?" she called in a quiet voice.

There it was again. "Please..." It sounded so sad.

"Tom, if that's you…"

"Please…"

Frances was frozen, her feet rooted to the floor in fear. The light had dimmed so much she couldn't see the end of the corridor. All she had to do was move, put one foot in front of the other.

"Please..."

A wave of cold blew across the back of Frances's neck. The next second, something brushed against her arm. She let out a scream and turned, the box in her arms crashing to the floor.

Tom looked up at her, pulling a face. "What's up with you?"

Warmth had spread through the corridor again, and it was full of light. Frances took a deep breath. "Nothing. Just felt a bit lost."

Tom rolled his eyes as he barged past, dragging a box of his own along the corridor. "You're just weird sometimes."

Frances knelt down and gathered up the CDs and books that had spilt out of the dropped box. Thankfully, her iPod dock was undamaged. She looked up and down the corridor. What was that about? Must have been her imagination.

She shivered again as she picked up the last of her things. All Frances could think about as she walked along the corridor was the sense of terror she had felt. A feeling that she hadn't been alone.

CHAPTER 2

Frances soon forgot about her spooky experience on that first day in the house. As the Brooks family settled into their new home, it felt like a distant memory. It must have been the heating pipes, or a draught blowing in through an open window somewhere.

Soon, it felt like they'd always lived at Stancliffe House. Boxes were gradually unpacked, pictures hung on walls and life went on as normal. They hadn't moved far from their old home, so for Frances and Tom, school remained the same.

They caught the bus as it passed the bottom of the lane, returning at the end of the day.

As they trudged up the lane from the bus stop, they passed Mrs Gardner's house. Sometimes the old lady would be standing in her garden, looking out over the valley, but they never said hello. They just kept their heads down and walked on towards home.

"She's weird," grumbled Tom.

Frances laughed. "You think everybody's weird."

"It saves time."

But there was something that stopped them from saying hello to their neighbour. It could have been shyness, but Frances knew that she felt uncomfortable around the old lady.

Mum popped her head round Frances's bedroom door. "Lights out."

Frances pulled her headphones out. "OK, Mum."

"What have I told you about having those things on in bed?"

"Erm…" Frances grinned. "Remind me?"

Mum shook her head, smiling back. "I swear, one of these days…"

"'Night, Mum."

"Sweet dreams!"

As Mum pulled her bedroom door closed, Frances switched off her bedside lamp and snuggled down under the duvet. She soon drifted off to sleep.

*

Frances sat up in bed. It was pitch black and her heart was hammering in her chest. Her eyes adjusted to the dark and picked out the lines of the bedroom furniture. Her breathing slowed, heartbeat returning to normal. She must have had a nightmare. Feeling silly, Frances pulled the duvet back over herself...

"Who's there?" She was bolt upright again, listening. There had been something... Yes! There it was again. Sobbing in the darkness.

Somebody was crying. A girl. Frances's eyes darted around the room, but she saw nothing in the murky black. The crying seemed to be coming from all around. Shivering, she pulled the duvet closer to her.

"Who are you?"

There was no answer, just stifled sobs.

"I can help you."

Whoever was crying, they sounded as scared as Frances was. "Please tell me who you are. Where you are."

The crying stopped. Frances listened, but the room was quiet apart from the sound of her own breathing. Then, it was there. A small, frightened voice in the dark.

"I'm sorry, Miss Hemlock. I'm sorry. I didn't mean to!"

*

When Tom woke up, he needed the toilet. He threw his duvet aside and padded to the door, which he opened as quietly as possible. He peered out. Moonlight fell through the window, casting silvery light on the landing. It made it look alien, and he liked that.

He crept out of his room and across the landing towards the bathroom. He passed his hands through the pale shaft of moonlight. He grinned when it turned silver, making him look like an alien robot.

A floorboard creaked. Tom turned quickly, looking back the way he had come. There was nothing there, just the landing, bedroom doors, and the rectangle of black at the top of the stairs. Tom laughed, nervously. He was starting to get like his sister, jumping at shadows.

He turned back and stepped towards the bathroom.

"I'm sorry."

Tom froze when he heard the voice.

"I'm so sorry."

Tom stubbed his toe against the wall as he looked round. He had definitely heard that. If this was his sister playing tricks, he'd...

"Please don't hurt me," the whispering voice pleaded. "I won't do it again, I promise."

Tom's mouth was dry. He wanted to ask who was there, but all that came out was a frightened croak. He took a step forwards, but stumbled backwards onto his bum when a shadow detached from the ink-black at the top of the stairs. It glided towards him and he could see it was a girl. She wore a long dress, and her flowing hair shone in the moonlight.

Tom put his hands up, as the pale figure seemed to pass straight through him.

"I'm so sorry, Miss Hemlock!"

The shadowy figure vanished, followed a second later by a terrifying, piercing scream. With a cry, Tom scrambled to his feet and dashed across the landing to Frances's room. He went in, slammed the door and stood with his back to it, breathing heavily and fighting back tears.

"Tom?"

Tom realised his sister's bedside lamp was on and she was sitting up in bed, her duvet pulled tight around her. She looked terrified.

"What is it?"

Tom went and sat on the edge of the bed.

"Think I just saw a ghost."

"You saw…?"

The bedroom light clicked on. Dad was standing at the door in his dressing gown, yawning. "Hey guys, what's going on?"

"Tom had a nightmare."

Tom protested. "So did Frances!"

"It's late. Go back to bed, OK?"

"OK Dad," said Frances.

Half asleep, Dad turned the light off and closed the door, leaving brother and sister in the light of the bedside lamp.

"You've seen something too, haven't you?" whispered Tom as soon as they heard their parents' bedroom door close.

Frances nodded. "More like heard."

As the night wore on, they began to tell each other about their ghostly experiences.

CHAPTER 3

"You two are quiet." Mum looked down at Frances and Tom where they sat at the breakfast table in the kitchen. They munched on toast and peanut butter.

Frances picked up a piece of toast. "Didn't sleep well."

Tom just mumbled through a mouthful of bread, almost too tired to speak.

"Early night for both of you tonight then." Mum picked up a basket of washing. "And get a shift on, you'll be late for the bus."

They both nodded as Mum left the room, but kept quiet.   As soon as they were alone, they leant close to each other so they could talk.

"Anything else happen last night?"

Tom shook his head. "I definitely saw it. A girl."

"I believe you." Frances thought for a moment. "Unless…"

"Unless what?"

"We haven't been here long. Maybe we're still getting used to the house." Frances shrugged. She didn't really believe that either.

"Yeah, 'cos all houses have screaming girls that can pass straight through people in them."

"Yeah, all right," said Frances, as Tom looked at her with his special 'big sisters are weird' look. "You've got a point."

"I'm soooo tired," moaned Tom, picking up his

plate and shuffling towards the sink, where he dumped it. He groaned. "Double maths first thing."

"French for me."

Tom stopped, his nostrils twitching.

Frances frowned. "What's up?"

Tom sniffed. "Can you smell burning?"

Frances took a breath through her nose. "Ugh. Burnt toast?"

Tom shook his head, wrinkling his nose against the sharp burning smell in the air. "Doubt it, we've finished eating."

"Tom!" Frances pointed towards the wall next to the dining table. Thick wisps of black smoke were forming out of thin air, rolling into billowing clouds. They both started to cough, as they were surrounded by the choking vapour. "Fire!"

"Where's it coming from?" Tom felt like crying.

"We've got to get out of here. Find Mum."

It was hard to see as the smoke wrapped itself around them. Their eyes watered and throats burned as they struggled to find the door. "Tom, come on!"

"I can't see you! Fran, I'm scared!"

"It's OK, we'll find a way out."

As quickly as it had appeared, the smoke vanished. Frances found herself standing in the middle of the room, arms outstretched towards Tom. The thick smoke had completely gone. Neither Frances nor Tom knew what to say. They could only look at each other in shock.

Tom wiped the tears from his eyes and knelt against the wall. He immediately jumped back. "Ow!"

Frances ran forward. "What?"

"The wall. It's hot!"

"Can't be." Cautiously, Frances reached out a
hand and touched the wall with her fingers. She
immediately snatched them back. It was hot.
Burning hot.

"See?" said Tom.

"It's the heating, must be."

"It's an outside wall."

Frances reached out a hand again. This time, the
wall was cold. Any trace of burning heat
was gone.

"Fran, what's going on?" Tom sounded small
and frightened.

"I don't know." Frances thought for a second.
"We should tell Mum and Dad. This is getting
too weird."

"Are you mad?" Tom shook his head. "They'll think we're the weird ones."

Frances sighed. He was probably right. All she knew was that something was very wrong at Stancliffe House.

"Come on. We're going to miss the school bus."

*

A light breeze was blowing across the valley when Frances and Tom jumped down from the school bus at the end of the day. As the bus roared away up the road, leaving engine fumes behind it, sister and brother walked slowly across the road towards home.

Frances was so tired she could barely keep her eyes open, and Tom looked pale.

"Think Mum'll let me go straight to bed?" asked Tom.

"Hello!" called a voice.

They'd reached the wall that bordered Mrs Gardner's lawn and their neighbour was walking quickly across the grass towards them. They both groaned, neither of them in the mood for an awkward conversation with an adult. Mrs Gardner smiled at them, then her expression changed to one of worry. She placed both hands on the stone wall and looked at them with those piercing blue eyes.

"Oh dear, you two don't look well."

"Just tired," replied Frances. Tom remained silent.

"Well, I may have just the thing for that. I've baked a chocolate cake, would you like to come in and have a slice? I get so lonely in this house all on my own sometimes."

"Thanks, but Mum'll have tea ready at home." Mrs Gardner's face fell in disappointment, so Frances added: "Sorry."

"Never mind," said Mrs Gardner. "Maybe next time."

Frances was about to reply when Tom blurted out, "I think our house is haunted!"

Mrs Gardner looked amused. "Do you now?"

"Yes." Tom looked about to burst into tears again, but held them back.

"Why do you say that?"

Before Tom could say anything else, Frances cut him off. "Mrs Gardner, did a girl use to live in our house?"

Mrs Gardner thought for a second. "A lot of people have lived in your house." The trace of a smile twitched at the corners of her mouth.

"But is it haunted?" Tom asked.

Mrs Gardner laughed. "I'm afraid I don't know. I've lived around here a long time and I can't recall ever seeing a ghost. But…" The old lady leant over the wall towards them, her bright blue eyes twinkling with humour. "Why don't you investigate the history of your new home?"

"Yeah, maybe."

Frances and Tom said goodbye and began their walk up the lane towards home.

"I'd love to know what you find out," Mrs Gardner called after them. The old lady had remained watching them as they walked away.

"Told you," said Tom unhappily. "She's weird."

CHAPTER 4

That night, Frances couldn't sleep. At any second she was expecting to hear whispering, or to be choked by thick, burning smoke. But the night was silent.

She woke with a gasp, having no idea how long she'd been asleep. It was still dark. Frances lay for a few seconds with her eyes closed, listening to the night. Somehow, she knew she wasn't alone.

"Help me."

Frances sat up in bed, switching her lamp on. "Who are you?"

"Help me." It was definitely a girl's voice.

Even with this ghostly voice calling out to her, Frances didn't feel frightened. "Where are you? I can't see you."

"Help me."

The voice was so quiet, seeming to move away across the room. Frances grabbed her dressing gown and tiptoed towards the door. Before she could think, Frances was out on the landing. It felt as if the voice was leading her somewhere.

"Help me."

"I'm coming," she whispered back. Should she get Tom? No, best to leave him where he was. He'd freak out at this.

"Help me."

Frances padded quietly down the stairs, not daring to make a sound. She felt excited and giddy as she followed the breathless voice. At the bottom of the stairs, she turned into the passageway that connected the hallway to the kitchen. The corridor where this had all begun.

"Help me." The voice was so quiet now she could barely hear it, but it seemed to have stopped halfway along the corridor. "Help me."

Frances was confused. "I don't know what you want me to do. How can I help?"

She walked towards where she thought the voice was. She stepped on a floorboard that rocked under her foot. It was loose! Kneeling, Frances found she could squeeze her fingers into the gap between the wooden boards. She heaved upwards, and felt the rusty nails give way.

Shaking a little, Frances felt into the space beneath the floorboard, her fingers brushing against something. She pulled out the object and tried to examine it in the darkness.

It was a book.

Frances and Tom stared down at the book on
the desk in Frances's room. Tom pulled a face.
"That's it? A book?"

"It's a diary." Frances gently picked up the
leather-bound book and opened it. "The pages
are all charred and burnt, but it's still just about
readable."

Frances read from the writing on the front page.
"'This diary is the property of Miss Victoria
Thomas of Stancliffe House.'"

They looked at each other. "The girl!" Tom
blurted out. "It must be."

A lot of the diary's pages were too blackened and
burnt to read, but towards the back they became
easier to make out. "'Wednesday 14 October,
1936,' Frances read aloud. "'Miss Hemlock
was in a foul temper today. I do not think my
governess likes me. She is cruel and teaches me

very little. She says I am wicked. I dare not tell Mother and Father about how she treats me as I do not think I will be believed.'"

"What's a governess?" asked Tom.

"Somebody who teaches you at home. Lots of posh families used to have them."

Frances carried on reading. "'Thursday 29 October, 1936. Miss Hemlock kept me locked in the schoolroom all day because I didn't get all my sums correct. I heard cook bring my lunch on a tray, but Miss Hemlock wouldn't let her in. Why does she hate me so much?'"

Tom pulled a face. "This Miss Hemlock sounds a right piece of work."

"'Monday 9 November, 1936. Miss Hemlock hit me this morning. She slapped me across the face, all the time calling me a wicked child. I think Father is beginning to realise what a monster she is, but perhaps it is too late. I think Miss

Hemlock is starting to hate this family. I fear what she might do to us.'" Frances looked up from the diary. "That was her last entry. The rest of the pages are blank."

Tom took the book from his sister and began to look through the crackling, fragile pages himself. "She sounded well scared."

"Not surprised with a governess like that," said Frances, frowning. "I wonder what happened to her? She just stopped writing." Tears shone in Frances's eyes. "I think something terrible happened."

"Could always find out." Frances looked on in confusion. "I've got an idea."

An hour later they were sitting in front of a computer in the big library in town. It was Saturday and they'd caught the bus, shouting something to Mum and Dad about having to finish a history project for school. Tom tapped at the keyboard.

"We came down here from school a few weeks back. They've got every issue of The Courier on a big hard drive somewhere. It's ace, you can search for anything."

Frances was almost too nervous to look for anything to do with Victoria or the house. She couldn't shake the feeling that something horrible had happened to her and her family. "Maybe we should leave it."

"Don't be daft. We're like time detectives, or something."

Frances laughed. "All right, you win. Start with Victoria Thomas."

Tom tapped in the letters and, seconds later, the screen flashed up with hundreds of links to articles. "That's too many."

"OK, try Victoria Thomas and Stancliffe House."

This time there were only five entries. Tom clicked on the first link. The front page of a

very old black-and-white edition of The Courier
appeared on the screen. As they read the
headline, their hearts sank.

6 DECEMBER, 1936

LOCAL FAMILY DIES IN HOUSE FIRE

The Thomas family of Stancliffe House, Boulder
Lane, were tragically killed when a section of their
home was destroyed by fire. Edward Thomas, his
wife Eleanor, and their daughter Victoria perished
in the blaze, which started in the early hours of 4
December. The cause of the fire is not yet known,
but local police are said to be questioning one Miss
Eliza Hemlock, the family governess. Miss Hemlock
was dismissed from service at the end of November;
acquaintances have alleged that she reacted
violently to the decision by Mr Thomas to remove
her from Stancliffe House. Investigations continue.

Frances and Tom sat quietly for a few moments,
taking in what they had just read. Tom broke the
silence. "So, she is a ghost."

CHAPTER 5

Frances felt sick as they got the bus home. She couldn't stop thinking about Victoria, her family, and what had happened at Stancliffe House.

It was 'spag bol' for tea, a family favourite, but both Tom and Frances had no appetite and just picked at it. Saturday night was usually family movie night, but Frances wasn't in the mood and Tom curled up on the sofa, reading his book.

"Everything OK, guys?" asked Dad. He had his worried face on. "You're alright with the new house, aren't you? You've both been a bit off since we moved in."

Mum said they both looked pale, maybe they were coming down with a cold. It was early, but neither of them argued when Mum packed them off to bed.

A little later, Tom crept into Frances's room. He sat on the end of her bed. "I can't stop thinking about her."

"Me neither. It's not fair. Miss Hemlock murdered them."

Tom shivered. "And here she is, haunting the house she was killed in."

"Do you really think she's a ghost?"

"What else could she be?"

Frances sighed. "I guess. It's still horrible."

"I wish we could talk to her."

Frances nodded sadly. A second later, her face brightened and she sat up in bed. "Maybe we can."

*

Frances opened her bedroom door a fraction and looked at the landing. It was dark and all was quiet. Her parents had gone to bed an hour before and she'd given them enough time to fall asleep before creeping out. She saw movement. Tom's head poked out from his room door. Frances pointed towards the stairs and he nodded.

Together, they crept down the staircase and into the hallway, neither speaking. Clutched in her hand, Frances could feel Victoria's diary. Somehow, it felt reassuring to have it with her.

"Are you sure about this?" whispered Tom behind her.

"No, but we have to try. You're the one that wanted to be a time detective, remember."

"That's in a book."

"Her ghost can talk to us. Makes sense we might be able to talk to her."

"Then what?"

Frances had to admit that Tom had her there. "Er... I don't know. Just shut up, OK?"

They had reached the hallway at the bottom of the stairs and were now standing at the end of the connecting corridor, darkness stretching out in front of them.

"Hang on." Tom fumbled for something and a narrow shaft of bright light shone into the corridor. "Never know when you'll need a torch."

Together, Frances and Tom stepped cautiously along the corridor.

"This is where I first heard the voice," explained Frances. "Where I found the diary." They stopped halfway down the corridor.

"Now what?" asked Tom.

Frances had no idea what she was doing as she knelt and placed the diary on the floor, but somehow it felt right. She stepped back and let Tom shine the torch onto it.

Frances's voice trembled when she spoke. "I don't know if you can hear me, but I'm Frances. This is my little brother, Tom."

"Hiya," said Tom, still shining the torch.

Nothing happened.

Frances tried again. "Victoria. Are you there?"

Just when she thought it was hopeless, a chill wafted down the corridor. Beside her, Tom shivered as it turned into a gentle breeze, the light from the torch shaking from side to side.

The diary suddenly sprang open, the charred pages fluttering in the icy draught.

"Fran," gulped Tom, his eyes wide with fear.

Frances put a hand on his shoulder. "It's OK."

Frances's skin prickled as the pages of the diary fluttered back and forth. She nearly jumped out her skin when a hand suddenly reached out from beyond the beam of light and closed the book. With a cry, Tom dropped the torch and it clicked off.

It didn't matter. Standing in a pale blue light in the middle of the corridor was a girl. She had long hair tied with a ribbon at the back, and wore a white dress with a lace collar. She held the diary close to her and looked with a mixture of wonder and fear at Frances and Tom.

"Who are you?" she asked. "If Miss Hemlock finds you here, we'll be punished."

"Are you Victoria?" asked Frances.

The girl cocked her head to one side. "That's right, Victoria Thomas." Nervously, she held out a hand. "I'm delighted to meet you, Frances and Tom."

Frances slowly held out her hand. Her fingers brushed against Victoria's, and then they were shaking hands. Victoria's hand was warm and definitely real. The girls smiled at each other.

"You're not a ghost!" Tom said.

Victoria frowned. "I hope not."

Frances couldn't believe it. "We kept hearing your voice, we thought you were a ghost."

"This is amazing!" said Tom. "It's a time corridor!"

"A what?" Frances and Victoria asked at the same time.

"A time corridor! It's in my books, where two points in time are connected. Brilliant!"

"I have absolutely no idea what you are talking about," laughed Victoria. Then her face crumpled with fear and she looked over her shoulder.

"Where are you, wicked child?" a strange voice said. It sounded a long way away, as if it were underwater. "Where are you?"

"Miss Hemlock!" gasped Victoria. She turned back to her new friends. "If she finds you here..."

Somewhere in the distance they heard heavy, thudding boot steps getting nearer and nearer.

Tom pointed at Victoria. "Fran, look at her!" She was starting to fade away.

"No!" said Frances, suddenly panicking. "Victoria, we have to warn you!"

"What's happening?" asked Victoria, panic in her blue eyes. "You're fading away."

"So are you!" Frances stepped forward. "Listen, Miss Hemlock does something terrible. When your father dismisses her, she tries to burn the house down!" Frances tried to take Victoria's hand, but they passed straight through each other. "Your mum and dad, they…"

Victoria's eyes locked with Frances's. "What? What about Mother and Father?"

"Child, I am coming for you!" Miss Hemlock's voice boomed horribly around the corridor, her thudding boot steps louder than ever now.

"Fran, I'm scared." Tom put his hand in his sister's.

Frances tried again. "Victoria, listen, you have to…"

It was too late. With one last look, Victoria turned away, as a shadow fell across the corridor. "No!" she gasped. "Please!"

Then she vanished.

CHAPTER 6

Victoria's diary sat once more on the desk in Frances's room. Frances sat on the bed, fighting back tears, while Tom stood and looked sadly at the book.

"If only we'd warned her earlier," said Frances. She was so angry with herself.

"We didn't know. Time's a tricky thing." Tom shrugged. "That's what it says in my books, anyway."

"This isn't a story, Tom. It's real."

"Yeah, I know. Sorry."

After that they didn't know what to say to each other. Tom yawned and realised he'd had no sleep. It would be morning soon. He was about to go when a sound stopped him. A crackling, fizzing sound. When he looked at the diary his eyes widened in amazement.

"Fran! Look at this!"

Frances wasn't sure she could put up with any practical jokes from her brother right now, but glanced over anyway. She blinked to clear her eyes to make sure she wasn't seeing things.

Victoria's diary was glowing!

Frances ran over to her desk. The diary was surrounded by an orange glow and, before their eyes, the burned edges of the book were repairing themselves. After a few more seconds, the glow vanished and the book was as good as new.

Brother and sister looked at each other in excited shock, before Frances picked up the diary and opened it. All the pages were free from any sign of fire damage, each page covered in neat handwriting. All the pages.

"Tom, the diary doesn't stop. Victoria keeps on writing."

"What does that mean?"

"It means," smiled Frances, "that we did it! We saved her!"

*

"You two seem a lot better," Mum said, as Frances and Tom laughed and joked with each other at breakfast on Sunday morning. The sun was shining and warmth spilled into the kitchen through the doors that opened onto the garden.

"We feel great, don't we Tom?"

"Yup!" Tom agreed with his sister. "This is the best house ever."

Dad laughed. "Glad to hear it." He glanced at the diary on the table next to Frances. "What you got there, love?"

Frances glanced at Tom and placed a hand on the diary. "Just some old book I found under a loose floorboard."

Dad nodded. "Old houses are great for that. Always full of history and stuff. You should go and show it to Victoria."

Tom stopped with a piece of toast halfway to his mouth, and Frances just stared. "Did you say Victoria?"

"Sorry. Mrs Gardner. She was telling us her family used to own this house. She lived here, back in the 1930s I think it was, before she got married."

Dad had barely finished speaking before Frances and Tom had raced out through the open doors.

*

"I wondered how long it would take you," Victoria Gardner smiled, cutting generous slices of chocolate cake and placing them before Frances and Tom. Her eyes – those sparkling blue eyes – twinkled with their usual mischief.

They were sitting out at the table in her garden, sunshine blazing down on them. Behind them, on the hillside, Stancliffe House stood looking over the valley.

Mrs Gardner – Victoria – had been waiting for them as soon as they had run down from Stancliffe House.

"When did you know?" asked Frances.

"That very first day, I'd have recognised you both anywhere. The two ghosts from the future who saved my life. And Mother's and Father's."

Tom looked at Mrs Gardner. "So, you're really old?"

"Tom!" said Frances, but Victoria laughed.

"Yes, I suppose I am."

Tom smiled. "You don't look it." He bit into his piece of chocolate cake.

"Thank you, Tom, that means a lot." She placed a hand over the cover of the diary. Her diary. "And thank you for bringing this back."

Frances was curious. "What happened to Miss Hemlock?"

"Miss Hemlock was a very disturbed person. But thanks to your warning on the night you appeared in the corridor, we were able to stop her from doing any harm. Father was able to arrange some help for her."

The three sat in silence for a few moments, enjoying the sunshine, until Victoria broke the silence. "I've been waiting a very long time for this moment, when I could thank my ghosts from the future for saving my family."

Frances and Tom smiled back at Victoria.

"I don't think she's weird any more," mumbled Tom through a mouthful of chocolate cake. Frances rolled her eyes, but Victoria laughed again and looked at both of them with her blue eyes.

"I can't wait for you to experience our next adventure together."

Frances looked at her questioningly.
"Next adventure?"

"Oh, yes," said Victoria mysteriously. "Our next adventure. Because the corridor through time never closes."

THE END